CW00923711

This book belongs to

....

Woody was an edgier, more aggressive character at first, before the creative team rethought his personality. **Bud Luckey and Ralph Eggleston / Marker and Pencil**

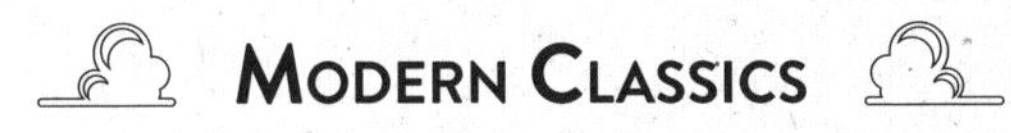

Disney • PIXAR

TOY STORY

Acknowledgments
Special thanks to Pixar Animation Studios and Walt Disney Animation Research Library for their invaluable assistance and for providing the artwork for this book.

First published in the UK in 2024 by Studio Press Books,
an imprint of Bonnier Books UK,
4th Floor, Victoria House, Bloomsbury Square,
London WC1B 4DA
Owned by Bonnier Books,
Sveavägen 56, Stockholm, Sweden
bonnierbooks.co.uk

Printed in China
2 4 6 8 10 9 7 5 3 1

ISBN 978-1-80078-733-9

Text adapted by Sally Morgan
Edited by Frankie Jones
Designed by Alessandro Susin
Cover illustrated by Chellie Carroll
Production by Giulia Caparrelli

A CIP catalogue record is available from the British Library

The first time I heard the words "Toy Story" was in 1993 and I was a senior in college. Graduation was a few months away and the animation department was abuzz for the school's annual Producers Show, an event where professionals in the industry met with students. If the studios liked what they saw in a student's work they might offer them a job.

I stood, in front of pages of my scribbles, nervously greeting anyone who passed by. Soon a familiar face walked up to me. My former professor, Joe Ranft. It had been years since we last spoke. He looked at my drawings with genuine interest. His approval felt like a million bucks.

Joe told me he was heading up the story team for Pixar Animation Studios where they had plans to make the first computer-animated feature film. Unfortunately, the filmmakers were in the middle of some massive re-writes and weren't hiring. But a year later Joe called me out of the blue, asking if I'd be interested in helping finish up the film. Soon after I met Andy's toys for the first time.

Joe became my mentor and continued to be a guiding force in my life. He taught me to 'Trust the Process', a philosophy we embrace at Pixar. Filmmaking is hard and a great story takes many years to develop. Our teams often go down many dead-ends before making any forward progress. Trusting the Process reminds us to embrace these trials.

Trusting the Process is the same lesson Woody has learned in the *Toy Story* films. He learned to trust the process of sharing the role of favourite toy and was rewarded with the reassurance of his owner's love. He learned to trust the process of enjoying each day, even though sometime in the future his kid may grow up and no longer need him. He even learned to trust that when that day finally does come, that Andy's affection was real and would always be with him. His final reward is a new home for him and his friends with Bonnie.

It has taken Woody and the toys four films to learn how to do it. For more than 30 years we at Pixar have worked to remember the lesson as well. As you read this, my hope is that you too find solace in the idea that when a problem presents itself you can slow down, rely on those around you to help and have faith that the solution will present itself in time. Trusting the Process is what Woody would do. Joe too.

Jason Katz
Story Supervisor
Pixar Animation Studios

In a bedroom filled with moving boxes, a young boy named Andy played with his toys. Andy liked to make up stories with his toys. In this adventure, One Eyed Bart, a Potato Head doll, attempted to rob the town bank which had been drawn onto the side of a box. A shepherdess doll tried to stop him, but One Eyed Bart told her to be quiet, or he would run over her sheep with race cars. Luckily, a hero was close at hand in the form of a cowboy toy named Woody.

"I'm here to stop you!" Andy said, giving Woody a voice. "Will you come quietly?"

One Eyed Bart didn't come quietly. Instead, he set his Slinky Dog on the cowboy. But Slinky Dog was no match for the plastic dinosaur Woody had brought with him. Woody's Dinosaur stomped on Slinky Dog. Woody told One Eyed Bart he was going to jail, and Andy picked up his Potato Head doll and put him behind the bars of his little sister Molly's crib, which he had labelled 'Jail'.

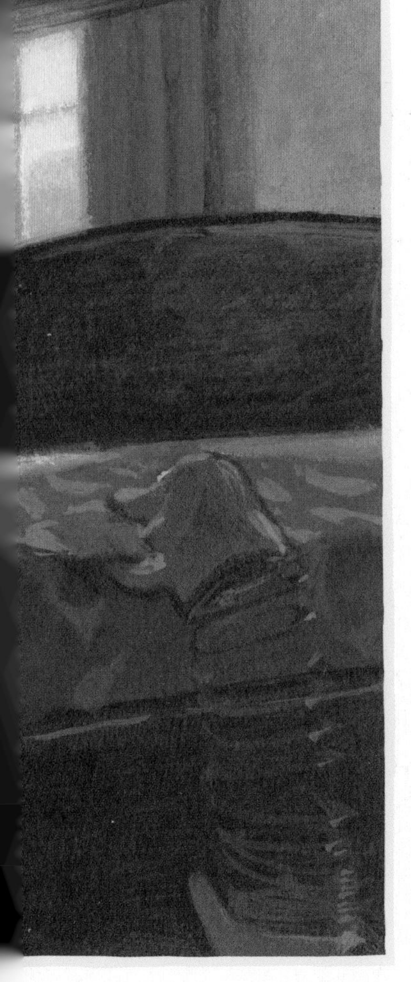

Andy said Woody had saved the day again, and pulled the string that made him speak.

"You're my favourite deputy," Woody recited.

Woody was Andy's favourite, too. Out of all of his toys, Andy played with Woody the most. Andy made Woody the star of all their adventures. They lassoed cattle, drove remote-controlled cars and played rough and tumble all over the house. Andy and Woody did everything together. But that was about to change.

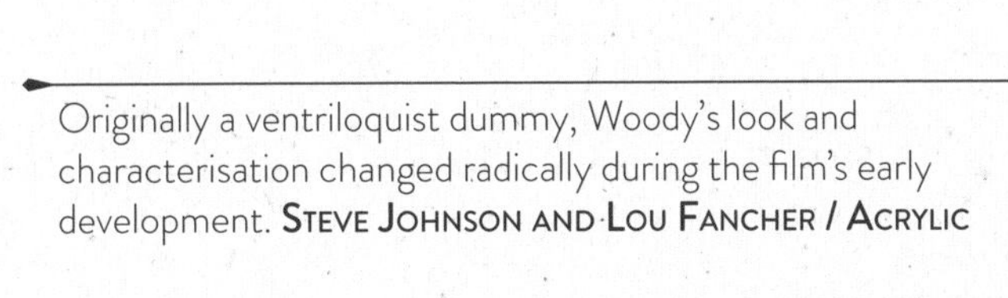

Originally a ventriloquist dummy, Woody's look and characterisation changed radically during the film's early development. **Steve Johnson and Lou Fancher / Acrylic**

While Molly tore Mr Potato Head apart in her crib, Andy took Woody downstairs where his mother was putting up decorations for his birthday party.

Andy asked if they could keep his decorations up until it was time to move house, and as that wasn't far off, his mother said they could. She then asked him to go and get his sister from upstairs because his friends would be arriving soon.

Andy raced upstairs. He tipped Woody's hat to say howdy to his sister before setting him down to get Molly out of her crib.

"See you later, Woody!" Andy said, closing the door behind him.

When Woody was sure Andy had gone, he sat up. Woody couldn't believe Andy's birthday party had caught him by surprise.

"Okay everybody. Coast is clear," Woody said, and Andy's bedroom sprung to life.

Toys emerged from the closet, climbed down from the shelves, and poked their heads out of the toy box. On the floor, Mr Potato Head gathered the pieces of himself that had been strewn about and complained that as he was designed for children who were older than three, he shouldn't have to babysit Andy's one-year-old sister.

"Have you seen Slinky?" Woody asked a plastic soldier named Sarge. Sarge saluted and said he had not. Woody hopped off the bed, as Slinky emerged from under it. The cowboy told Slinky that he had bad news, and asked Slinky to help him gather all the toys together.

Slinky Dog's southern hound dog personality is in part inspired by voice actor Jim Varney's own dog, who sometimes seemed to be trying to speak. **TIA W. KRATTER AND RALPH EGGLESTON / ACRYLIC**

“Staff meeting, everybody,” Woody called. Woody directed Snake and Robot toy to build a podium for him, while he went in search of his doodle pad. Woody found it by Andy’s desk, but before he could grab it, Rex the dinosaur leapt out at him and roared. Woody barely looked up.

Sheriff Woody has always had a soft spot for porcelain shepherdess Bo Peep in the *Toy Story* films. **MICHAEL YATES / DIGITAL**

Rex asked Woody if he had been scared. Rex was worried that he was more annoying than scary. Woody assured him that he was, almost.

Woody headed back to the podium but was stopped by Bo Peep, who pulled him over to thank him for saving her sheep. Woody giggled bashfully, and assured her it was nothing. Bo Peep said if Woody wanted to get together, he knew where to find her. Woody gazed after her as she left.

"Hey Woody! C'mon!" Slinky said, bringing Woody back to his senses.

At the podium, Woody checked if everyone could hear him okay before he began. The first item for discussion was whether each of the toys had a moving buddy. Andy's family was due to move house in one week, and Woody wanted to make sure that no toy was left behind.

The next item on the agenda was one Woody knew would cause a stir.

"Andy's birthday party's been moved to today," Woody said, under his breath. Woody tried to move on, but the toys had descended into panic.

Rex asked why Andy's party was today, when his birthday wasn't until next week. Woody said it was probably because Andy's mother didn't want the party to get in the way of the big move.

Many of Andy's toys are based on vintage toys. Woody's design took inspiration from the Howdy Doody puppets of the 1950s.
BUD LUCKEY / PENCIL

Woody told the toys that he wasn't worried, but Mr Potato Head replied that, unlike the rest of them, Woody was Andy's favourite and was unlikely to be replaced. Woody said that that wasn't the point – their job as toys was to be there for Andy, no matter what.

Soon the guests arrived, and the toys rushed to the window to see what gifts they carried. Hamm worried that they would all be put out for a garage sale. As more presents arrived, the toys grew more worried. Woody asked if they would calm down if he sent the toy soldiers to see what was going on. The toys agreed that they would.

Woody told Sarge it was a code red. Sarge knew just what to do, and soon a troop of soldiers marched towards the door carrying a baby monitor and a skipping rope. On the landing, Sarge watched Andy's mother direct the guests into the living room, before he signalled his men to parachute down. The parachutists then signalled that it was safe to follow using the rope. The soldiers froze when Andy's mother appeared from the kitchen with chips.

Andy stores his 200 miniature green plastic soldiers in a bucket labelled 'Bucket O' Soldiers'. **Joe Ranft / Pencil**

The Green Army Men are led by Sarge and have a 'leave-no-man-behind' policy.
RALPH EGGLESTON / PASTEL

"Owww!" she gasped, stepping on one of them.

In the bedroom, the toys waited impatiently around the monitor for news.

Downstairs, the stepped-on soldier told the rest to carry on without him, but Sarge helped him up and signalled the upstairs soldiers to lower the baby monitor into a plant. When the monitor and the wounded soldier were safely concealed in the plant, Sarge positioned himself to watch as Andy opened his first present.

In the bedroom, static crackled through the monitor. "This is it!" Woody said, as the broadcast began.

Woody describes the Green Army Men as 'professionals' and sends them to report back on the gifts Andy receives for his birthday. **Ralph Eggleston / Pastel**

Sarge told the toys that Andy was opening his first present. Mr Potato Head wished out loud for a Mrs Potato Head, but it was a lunchbox. The toys were relieved. The next present was a new set of bed sheets.

"Who invited that kid?" Mr Potato Head joked.

As Andy worked his way through his gifts the tension subsided until relief flooded the bedroom when Sarge announced that the last gift was a game of Battleship.

Woody said he had told them they had nothing to worry about.

But downstairs, Andy's mother pulled a surprise present from the closet. The toys in the bedroom tensed when the monitor came back on and Sarge announced there was another large present. Sarge tried to see what it was, but children kept getting in his way.

In the bedroom, Rex was desperate to know what it was. He grabbed the nightstand and accidentally knocked the monitor to the ground, dislodging its batteries. Mr Potato Head tried to reinsert them while Woody hopped off the bed to help.

Downstairs, done with his presents, Andy asked his friends up to his room to play. The children rushed past Sarge in the hall and up the stairs.

"Red alert!" Sarge warned, but the toys couldn't hear the monitor. When Woody finally reinserted the batteries, Sarge's voice blasted a warning and Woody told the toys to get to their places. The toys scattered in a panic.

When the door to the bedroom flew open and the children rushed in, Woody lay limp on the bed, just where Andy had left him.

Woody developed from a ventriloquist doll into a loose-limbed cowboy doll, which helped reduce the scale differences between him and Buzz. **Bud Luckey And Ralph Eggleston / Pencil**

Andy's friends cleared the bed to make space for the new toy and Woody slid off the blanket. Andy showed off his toy until his mother called them for party games and the children tore out in a stampede.

As quiet descended, Andy's toys moved towards the bed to meet the new toy.

"Who's up there with you?" Rex called, thinking Woody was still on the bed.

The toys were shocked when Woody crawled out from under the bed.

Mr Potato Head said the new toy had taken Woody's place on the bed and Rex asked if he had been replaced.

Woody assured the toys that no one had been replaced, and that they must give the toy a warm welcome. He climbed up the blanket and gulped when he saw an action figure, wearing a flashy spacesuit, covered in buttons and stickers.

As the figure came to life, it pressed one of its buttons.

"Buzz Lightyear to Star Command," Buzz said. He looked around, and found his spaceship box on Andy's pillow. Buzz spoke into the arm of his spacesuit to log that he had crashed on a strange planet with no sign of intelligent life.

At that moment, Woody peered around Buzz's visor and said hello.

Buzz yelled, and aimed his laser at Woody. Woody apologised for startling him and welcomed him to Andy's room. Woody then explained that the bed was usually his spot.

Buzz introduced himself as a space ranger from the Universe Protection Unit and said his ship had crashed by mistake. Woody was relieved Buzz recognised the mistake.

Suddenly, Buzz threw Woody to the ground, and fired his laser at the edge of the bed.

"Who goes there?" Buzz yelled.

In this early concept art, Buzz Lightyear's space ranger costume has red and yellow highlights, instead of the blue and green shades that he ended up with. **BUD LUCKEY / CONCEPT ART**

It was Rex and Slinky. Buzz asked Woody if he knew them. Woody, annoyed to have been thrown down, said they were Andy's toys. Buzz introduced himself.

Rex asked what the buttons on Buzz's suit did. Buzz pressed one, and a recorded voice announced, "Buzz Lightyear to the rescue". Slinky told Buzz that Woody had a voice too, but Mr Potato Head said that Woody's voice sounded like a car had run over it.

Hamm asked whether Buzz had been made in Hong Kong or Singapore. Buzz said that he was from Sector Four, and was part of a force that protected the galaxy from Evil Emperor Zurg.

As Buzz spoke, Woody noticed that Buzz was using the exact words printed on the side of his spaceship box.

"You'd think they'd never seen a new toy before," Woody muttered to Bo Peep.

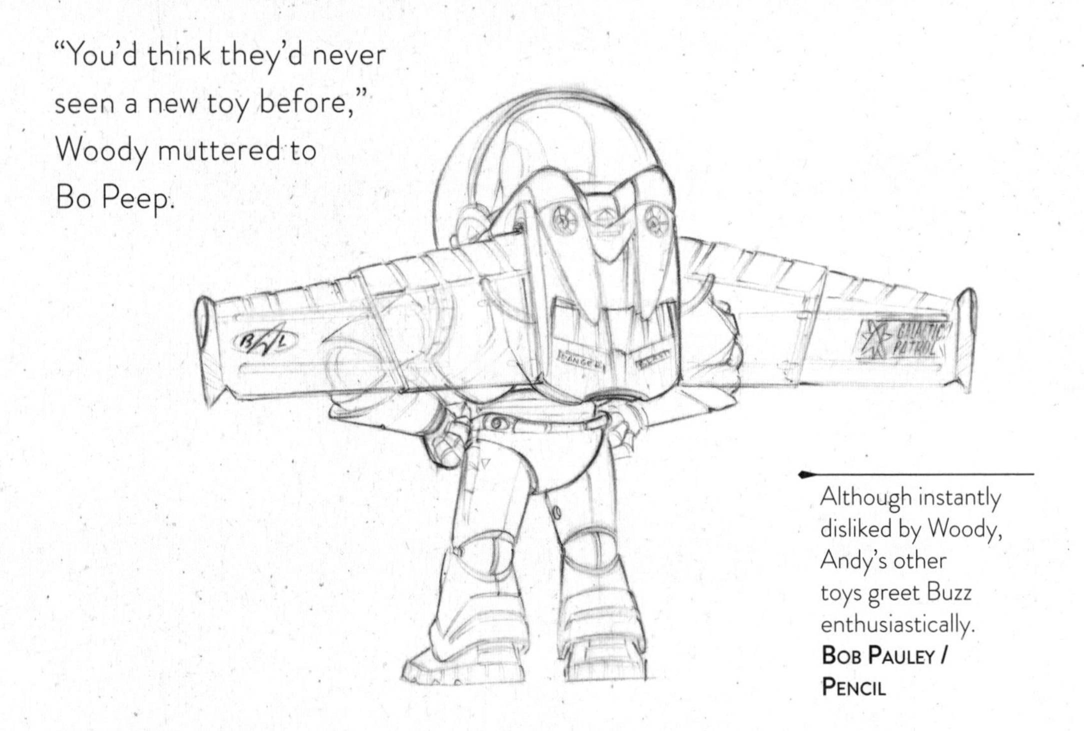

Although instantly disliked by Woody, Andy's other toys greet Buzz enthusiastically. **Bob Pauley / Pencil**

As a money bank, Hamm is not technically a toy, but the animators gave him toy-like movements and a character to match. **RALPH EGGLESTON / PENCIL**

Bo Peep said Buzz was getting so much attention because his spacesuit was covered in gadgets.

Slinky tried one of Buzz's buttons next. Buzz told them to be careful as they could set off his laser. Mr Potato Head asked Woody why he didn't have a laser. Annoyed, Woody pointed out that Buzz's was just a lightbulb.

Mr Potato Head accused Woody of laser envy.

Woody said he understood that everyone was very impressed with the new toy.

"Toy?" Buzz repeated. He asked if Woody meant to say space ranger.

Woody was annoyed, but Rex wanted to know what a space ranger did.

"He's not a space ranger," Woody huffed, and said that Buzz could not shoot lasers or fly.

Andy's childhood drawings adorn the walls of his bedroom. **Ralph Eggleston / Concept Art**

Woody grabbed Buzz's wing and said it was plastic, and could not fly. But Buzz boasted that he could fly around the room with his eyes closed. Woody told him to prove it. Buzz asked everyone to stand back. He walked to the edge of the bed and climbed up Andy's bed post. Buzz closed his eyes.

"To infinity and beyond," Buzz cried, and leapt. He fell, but bounced off a ball. When Buzz began to fall again, he landed on a toy car. Buzz rode the car down the steep track and whizzed off the end, only to become hooked on an aeroplane tacked to Andy's ceiling. The aeroplane swung Buzz around before dropping him back onto the bed.

Buzz thanked the toys, who clapped and cheered. Woody was not impressed. "That wasn't flying!" Woody complained. "That was... falling with style."

Woody told Slinky that soon everything would go back to normal and everyone would see that he was still Andy's favourite toy.

But over the next few days, things in Andy's room changed. Instead of Woody, Andy made Buzz the hero in his games. Andy swapped his cowboy posters for pictures of Buzz, and instead of wearing his cowboy hat, Andy made a helmet and wings from cardboard.

The toys warmed to Buzz, too. Buzz helped Rex with his roar, styled Troll's hair, and scratched Slinky's chin until he wagged his tail in Woody's face. At the end of the day, instead of settling down next to Andy, Woody watched sadly from the toybox as his old friend got tucked up under a Buzz Lightyear blanket, with Buzz by his side.

Woody struggles with being upstaged by a shinier, newer toy. **BUD LUCKEY / PENCIL**

When Woody woke the next morning, Buzz was already up and talking to Rex and Slinky by the drawers. Buzz showed them Andy's name written on his foot. Rex was impressed that Andy had used permanent ink.

Woody looked at his own foot, to check Andy's name was still there. Bo Peep came to his side. She said Andy would always have a special place for Woody. "Like the attic," Mr Potato Head joked.

Buzz's stock phrase "To infinity and beyond!" has become an iconic catchphrase, synonymous with the character.
Bob Pauley / Marker and Correction Fluid

Andy's toys look forward to moving to escape Sid and his toy-terrorising ways.
Dan Haskett / Pencil

But Woody had had enough. When Woody found Buzz, he was repairing his ship. Woody told Buzz to stay away from Andy. But all Buzz cared about was repairing his spaceship. Buzz asked the toys for more tape.

Woody told Buzz to stop pretending to be a spaceman, because it got on his nerves. Buzz asked Woody if he wanted to complain to Star Command. Woody thought Buzz was making fun of him, and challenged him to a fight. As Woody pushed Buzz, he hit a button. Buzz's helmet flipped open and Buzz struggled to breathe. Buzz fell to his knees before he realised the air was fine.

"How dare you open a spaceman's helmet!" Buzz said.

Woody asked if Buzz thought he was a real spaceman. Woody believed Buzz had been putting on an act, but he was not. Woody called everyone over to laugh at Buzz.

"You are mocking me, aren't you?" Buzz asked. Woody lied and said he was not.

From outside, the toys heard a dog barking and a child shouting. The noise sent Slinky to hide under the bed. "Oh no, not Sid!" Rex said as the toys rushed to the window.

Down below, Andy's neighbour, Sid, played with his dog. Mr Potato Head asked if Sid had a toy with him.

Through Lenny the binoculars, Woody saw Combat Carl with a firework strapped to his back. Buzz asked what was going on. Woody told him it was a matter for toys, not 'spacemen'. Rex explained that Sid tortured toys for fun.

Down below, Sid lit the firework. The toys leapt for cover as the explosion shook the house. Combat Carl was gone and Sid laughed.

"I could have stopped him," Buzz muttered. Woody said he would love to see Buzz try, or to see him become a crater.

***

The following evening, Andy was playing with Woody and Buzz in his room, piled high with boxes, when his mother put her head around the door to ask if he wanted to go to Pizza Planet.

Andy left his toys on the desk. When Andy left the room, Woody heard Andy ask if he could bring toys. Andy's mother said he could bring one.

Woody asked the Magic Eight Ball if Andy would choose him.

"Don't count on it." Woody threw the ball off the desk. He watched it fall, then looked at Buzz.

"Buzz!" Woody called. Woody told Buzz that a toy was trapped behind the desk and needed help. Buzz ran to the edge to look for it. Meanwhile, Woody picked up the controls of the remote-control car.

"I don't see anything!" Buzz said, his back to Woody. Woody steered the car at Buzz to knock him down. Buzz leapt out of the way.

RC Car knocked the noticeboard, which set the globe rolling towards Buzz. Buzz ran to the windowsill as the globe rolled into Andy's angle lamp, which swung and knocked Buzz out of the window.

"Buzz!" Woody called after him.

The relationship between Woody and Buzz gets off to a rocky start before growing into a deep friendship. **RALPH EGGLESTON / PASTEL**

Early in character development, Woody wasn't immediately likeable. The team made him more sympathetic, but as top toy he's still a little selfish. **Bud Luckey / Pencil and Correction Fluid**

The toys looked down, but they couldn't see Buzz. Woody backed away, but RC Car revved loudly.

Translating for RC, Mr Potato Head said that Buzz hadn't fallen, but was pushed out of the window by Woody. The toys gasped.

Woody told the toys it was an accident. Slinky believed him, but Rex didn't know what to think. Mr Potato Head said that Woody got rid of Buzz because he was jealous and didn't like not being Andy's favourite toy any more. Mr Potato Head asked Woody if he would do the same to him.

Woody wanted to explain, but before he could, the toys heard Andy say he was going to get Buzz and hurried to their places.

When Andy entered, he couldn't find Buzz. It was time to go, but Andy didn't want to leave without him. Andy's mother told him to choose another toy. Andy picked up Woody and left to get in the car.

Unseen by the toys upstairs, Buzz watched as Andy carried Woody to the car. When Andy's mum started the engine, Buzz raced to the car and grabbed the bumper before it pulled away.

In Andy's room, the toys lowered a chain of monkeys to rescue Buzz, but it was not long enough. Rex called down to where he thought Buzz might be and told him to stay calm.

***

On the road, Andy's mother stopped to get petrol. Andy and his mother climbed out of the car. Alone, Woody wondered aloud how he was going to convince the toys that what happened was an accident. Woody looked up and saw Buzz staring at him through the sunroof.

The Dinoco gas station features in other Pixar movies. **RALPH EGGLESTON / PASTEL**

Woody was delighted. If Buzz was okay, he could tell the toys it was all a big mistake. But Buzz did not think it was a mistake. Buzz knew that Woody had pushed him. Buzz lunged and threw them both out of the window. The action figures fought, unaware that Andy was back. The toys stopped fighting just in time to see Andy and his mother drive away.

Buzz's belief that he's a space ranger and not a toy creates friction between himself and Woody.
Ralph Eggleston / Pastel

"I'm a lost toy!" Woody sobbed and fell to his knees. Behind him, Buzz calmly observed the situation. Woody's despair turned into white hot rage. Woody ran at Buzz, but fell to the ground when caught in the beam of a lorry's headlights. Buzz dived out of the way and the lorry halted just centimetres from Woody's nose.

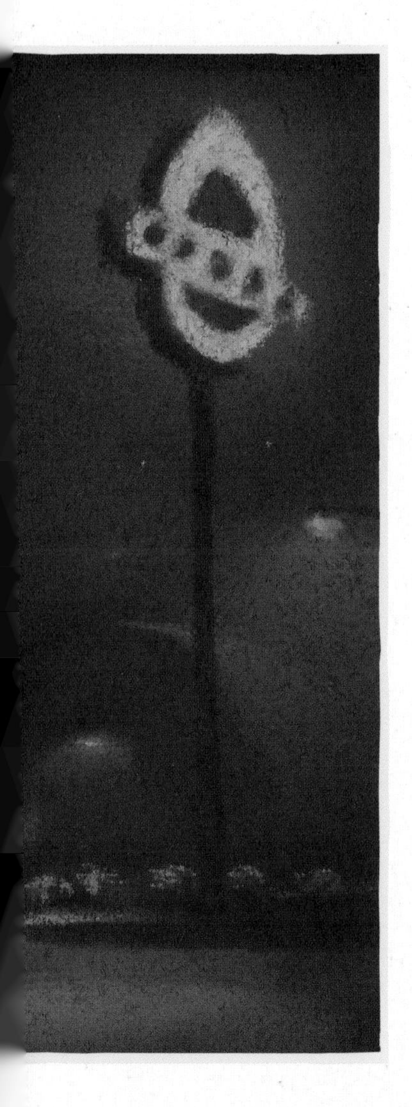

Woody edged away from the enormous wheel, and bumped into Buzz, who was adding the latest incident to his log. Woody told him to shut up. Buzz replied that this was no time to panic. Woody thought losing Andy two days before he moved was the exact time to panic, and that it was all Buzz's fault for showing up and taking away everything that was important to him.

Buzz said they were lost because of Woody, and what Woody had done had put the whole universe in danger.

"What are you talking about?" Woody asked.

Buzz pointed at the stars, and explained that Emperor Zurg was building a planet-destroying weapon, and that he was the only ranger who could defeat him. Woody's actions had stopped him from returning to Star Command.

"You... are... a... toy!" Woody yelled.

Buzz told Woody that he pitied him, and said goodbye.

"Good riddance, you loony," Woody called after him. Woody was still muttering to himself when a delivery vehicle pulled in. Woody read the words written on the side.

"Pizza Planet," Woody gasped. Woody ran towards it, but stopped. He couldn't face the toys without Buzz. Woody called Buzz to come back, but Buzz told him to go away. Woody looked at the delivery vehicle, and noticed that it had a Pizza Planet rocket ship on the roof.

Woody told Buzz he had found a spaceship. Woody said that when the vehicle finished delivering pizzas, it would go back to its point of origin where they would find a way to get Buzz home.

"Let's climb aboard," Buzz said, and walked towards the passenger door. Woody thought they should ride in the back, but Buzz didn't want to ride without a seatbelt. Buzz swung himself through the window and sat next to the pizzas. Woody tried calling out to him, but when he heard the engine, ran to the back and climbed in.

"What an idiot," Woody muttered as Buzz strapped himself in, but when the driver pulled away, Woody was thrown and got crushed by a toolbox.

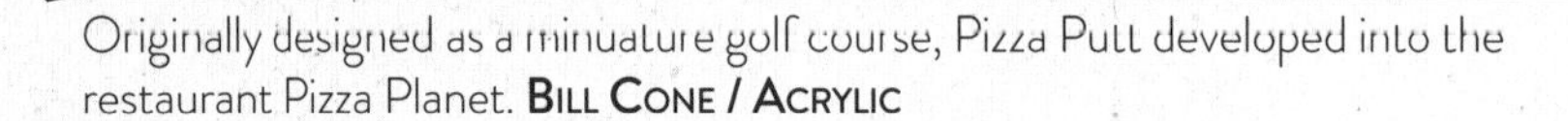

Originally designed as a minuature golf course, Pizza Putt developed into the restaurant Pizza Planet. **Bill Cone / Acrylic**

When they arrived at Pizza Planet, Buzz looked out and saw the entrance had animatronic guards. Buzz watched the guards raise their pizza-tipped spears to allow customers to enter.

Buzz found Woody under the toolbox. He told Woody that they needed a way to get past the guards. Dazed, Woody pulled a paper cup off his head to listen. Believing the cup was a disguise, Buzz said that he liked Woody's thinking.

Moments later, wearing a drink cup and a burger box, Woody and Buzz followed a family through the doors and hid behind an arcade machine. "Where's the spaceport?" Buzz asked, looking around, when Woody heard a familiar voice. It was Andy!

But Buzz wanted to find a spaceship. Woody lied, saying he knew where to find one. Buzz asked if it had hyperdrive, and Woody confirmed that it did. Woody told Buzz to jump into Molly's stroller as it passed. Instead, Buzz ran the other way towards a rocket-ship claw machine and leapt inside.

Buzz climbs inside the claw machine, believing it to be a rocket which will take him to his destination. **Kelly Asbury / Marker and Pencil**

"This cannot be happening to me!" Woody complained as he left Andy to chase Buzz.

Inside the machine, Buzz was surrounded by Alien toys. "I come in peace," Buzz said, as the Aliens crowded around.

Woody followed the sound of Buzz's voice. Buzz asked who was in charge and the Aliens pointed to the claw. The Aliens said the claw chose who would stay and who would leave. Suddenly, Woody heard another familiar voice. It was Sid.

"Get down!" Woody leapt on Buzz to hide while Sid fished for a coin.

The Squeeze Toy Aliens live inside a claw vending machine. They worship the claw as a deity who they believe selects Aliens to go to a better place. **JASON KATZ / MARKER AND PENCIL**

Buried among the Aliens, Buzz and Woody watched the claw lift an Alien to the prize chute.

"Gotcha," Sid whispered, before spying Buzz.

Woody looked for an escape, and found a door at the back of the machine. The claw whirred, and Woody looked back to see it close around Buzz. Woody tried to pull Buzz towards the door, but the Aliens stopped him. The Aliens helped the claw lift Buzz and Woody and drop them into the prize chute.

"Let's go home and play," Sid laughed cruelly, fishing out the toys.

When Sid got back, Buzz saw Andy's house from the backpack and told Woody he would be home soon. The Alien was excited too as it believed it had been chosen for something special. Woody told them that once inside Sid's house there was no coming out alive.

Scud greeted Sid at the door, barking. Sid pulled out the Alien toy and balanced it on Scud's nose. Scud flipped the toy into his mouth and shook it hard.

Sid's room is littered with disturbing artefacts, including threatening posters and torture equipment. **STEVE JOHNSON AND LOU FANCHER / ACRYLIC**

Sid asked his sister, Hannah, if she'd seen a package for him. Hannah hadn't. Sid snatched her doll, Janie, and said she needed an operation. "Don't touch her!" Hannah cried. She chased Sid up the stairs, and begged him to give Janie back. Sid laughed, and slammed the door.

Sid threw his backpack onto his bed and went to his workbench. He asked an imaginary nurse to prepare his operating theatre. Woody and Buzz watched Sid clamp Janie's head in a vice.

Hannah said she was going to tell their mother, but Sid continued with the operation he called a double bypass brain transplant. He grabbed a pterodactyl from a junk box.

When Sid was done, he took Janie to Hannah and said she was better. Hannah screamed. Sid had replaced the doll's head with that of the pterodactyl. Hannah ran to tell her mother and Sid ran after her, yelling that she was a liar.

With Sid gone, Buzz and Woody looked around the room and shuddered. Sid's room was a museum dedicated to his monstrous toy operations.

"I'm out of here," Woody said. Woody dashed to the door, but it was locked.

Sid's idea of fun is terrorising his little sister and performing experiments on her toys.
Ralph Eggleston / Pastel

Woody looked for a way out, but got spooked by strange noises. Sensing something moving, Woody picked up a flashlight, and shone it under the bed.

"Hi there, little fella," Woody said, when he saw part of a doll's face. Woody asked if it knew a way out. But as the face drew closer, Woody saw that it sat on top of a mechanical spider and had only one eye.

Woody turned and saw other monstrous mashups – a fishing pole with fashion-doll legs, a jack-in-the-box with a pop-up hand and a rolling toy with the head of an action figure. Woody ran and hid behind Buzz.

Woody and Buzz climbed back into the backpack. Woody sat trembling as Buzz reset his laser from stun to kill. Woody joked that if the laser didn't work, they could blink the toys to death.

Next door, the toys watched Andy's mother pull into the driveway.

"Mom, have you seen Woody?" Andy asked as he got out of the car. Andy was sure the last place he had him was in the back of the car. "Woody's gone," Andy said.

"Woody's gone?" Bo Peep asked. Mr Potato Head and Hamm said Woody had run away because he was guilty.

But Bo Peep was worried and hoped Woody was okay.

The next morning, Sid woke early to play. "We have ways of making you talk," Sid said, pretending to interrogate Woody.

Sid used a magnifying glass to concentrate a beam of sunlight on Woody's head. Sid laughed as Woody's head started to smoke.

The mutant toys are made from mixed pieces of toys that belong to Sid and his sister, Hannah. **Bud Luckey / Pencil**

“Sid, your Pop Tarts are ready,” Sid’s mother called from downstairs. Sid dropped the magnifying glass, and ran.

When Sid was gone, Woody yelled in agony, and dunked his head into a cereal bowl. Buzz stumbled over to see if he was okay.

Woody examined his head in the back of a spoon and saw in the reflection that Sid’s door was open. Woody ran towards it, but before he got there, his path was blocked by mutant toys. Buzz aimed his laser at them, but didn’t understand why it wasn’t working.

Sid’s treatment of toys contrasts with Andy who loves and cares for his toys. **Bud Luckey / Pencil**

The Buzz Lightyear commercial is inspired by fast-paced 1990s toy commercials.
RALPH EGGLESTON / PASTEL

Woody told Buzz to use his karate chop, and activated it using a button on Buzz's back. Buzz didn't understand how Woody was able to make his arm move. Woody walked out of the door using Buzz, and his karate chop, as a shield.

Woody ran down the stairs, but stopped when he saw Scud asleep on the landing. Woody crept back up the stairs. At the top Buzz told him that he could have had them both killed. Woody followed Buzz across the landing quietly, but his pull cord caught on the baluster and let out a loud 'giddy-yap'. Scud growled as he came up the stairs. Woody and Buzz split up to escape. Buzz darted into a room where a man lay in a recliner, watching television. Scud pushed his nose around the door, but a sudden snore from the chair sent him running away. Buzz flipped open his communicator to call Star Command, when he heard his name coming from the television.

Buzz looked at the screen, and saw an advert for a Buzz Lightyear that looked just like him. The voiceover described all of Buzz's special features, before showing a picture of Buzz with the words 'Not a flying toy', in bold letters. The advert ended inside a store filled with hundreds of Buzz Lightyears stacked in spaceship boxes. Buzz opened his communicator and read the words 'Made in Taiwan'.

Buzz wandered into the hall. He looked out of the window at a bird and remembered what Woody had said. He was a toy, and he could not fly. Buzz didn't want to believe it. He climbed up the stair railings, popped open his wings, and fixed his gaze on the sky.

"To infinity and beyond!" Buzz declared, and leapt. But he did not glide through the window – he fell. On the ground, Buzz saw his arm had detached.

Buzz was still lying in the entryway when Hannah came looking for her Sally doll, and stepped on him. Hannah picked Buzz, and his arm, up from the floor.

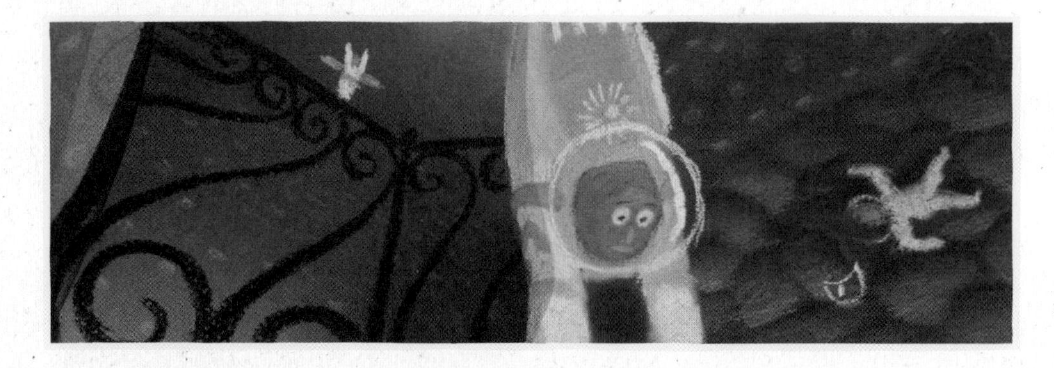

Buzz's last failed attempt at flight sees him fall down the staircase at Sid's house.
Ralph Eggleston / Pastel

Buzz is shaken when he discovers he is a toy, not a space ranger. **Bud Luckey / Pencil**

Upstairs, Woody hid inside a closet. He jiggled the door handle, and fell out. "Oof!" Woody yowled as a bowling ball landed on his head. Woody called out for Buzz, but Buzz didn't answer. Instead, Woody heard Buzz's preprogrammed voice coming from down the hall. Tangled in lights from the closet, Woody went in search of Buzz and found him wearing a pink apron, and a flowery hat.

"Would you like some tea, Mrs Nesbitt?" Hannah asked as she poured pretend tea into Buzz's cup.

"Oh no!" Woody said.

In the hall, Woody called Hannah's name in a high-pitched voice. Thinking it was her mother, Hannah left to see what she wanted.

"Buzz, are you okay?" Woody asked. But Buzz was drunk on imaginary tea. Buzz told Woody that he was Mrs Nesbitt, and started laughing. Woody hit him with his detached arm.

"I'm sorry," Buzz said, coming round. Buzz said he was depressed, and would get through it, but in the hall Buzz started crying loudly and told Woody about trying to fly through the window.

"Buzz, you're a genius," Woody said.

In Andy's room, Mr Potato Head and Hamm heard a familiar voice outside. "It's Woody," Hamm called. The toys gathered around the window and saw Woody waving from Sid's room.

Woody threw one end of a string of Christmas lights over and asked the toys to tie it to something, so that he could climb across. But Mr Potato Head asked the toys if they wanted Woody back, after what he had done to Buzz.

Woody told the toys that Buzz was fine. Woody called Buzz over to tell them he wasn't dead, but Buzz didn't move. Woody asked Buzz to give him a hand, and Buzz threw up his arm. "Very funny," Woody said. Woody begged Buzz, and told him it was serious, but Buzz didn't care.

Woody was desperate. Woody took Buzz's arm to the window and used it to wave at the toys. "Hiya fellas!" Woody said, mimicking Buzz's voice. Mr Potato Head asked Woody what he was trying to pull. Woody raised his hands to prove he had nothing to hide, but instead revealed that Buzz's arm was not attached to Buzz.

Andy's toys are shocked when they realise Woody is holding Buzz's dismembered arm. **RALPH EGGLESTON / PASTEL**

Bo Peep screamed and Mr Potato Head called him a murdering dog. Woody tried to explain that Buzz was fine and that he needed their help to escape Sid, but the toys had seen enough. Mr Potato Head let the end of the lights drop as they walked away. Woody begged Slinky, his most loyal friend, to listen to him, but Slinky pulled down the blind.

As dark clouds rolled in overhead, Woody heard a clattering sound behind him. Woody turned to see Buzz surrounded by Sid's mutant toys. Woody rushed to shoo them away, but they wouldn't leave. Instead, the baby-faced spider took Buzz's arm from Woody. Woody tried to pull the toys off Buzz. He thought they were monsters, and told them that he wouldn't let them eat Buzz, but when they stepped aside, Woody saw that instead of eating him they had reattached his arm.

The mutant toys show Woody and Buzz they are friendly by reattaching Buzz's arm.
Ralph Eggleston / Pastel

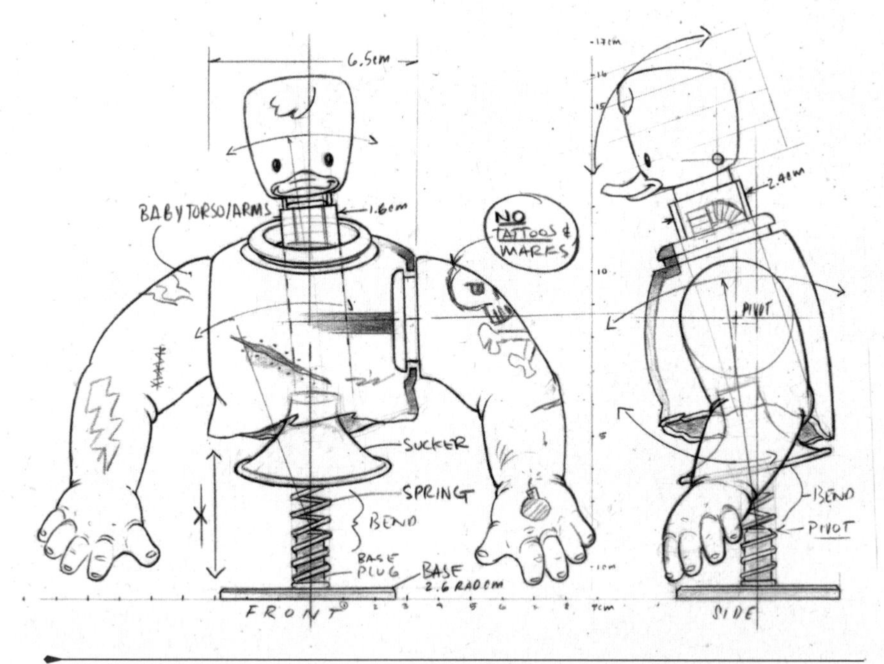

Ducky is a mutant toy made from a candy dispenser atop a baby doll torso with a plunger base. **BOB PAULEY / PENCIL**

"Hey. They fixed you," Woody marvelled. "But they're cannibals!" Woody apologised for what he said, but as he approached, they hid under the bed. Woody tried to call them back, but they weren't hiding from Woody – Sid was on his way. Woody tried to pull Buzz to safety, but Buzz wouldn't move. Woody managed to hide under a crate, just as Sid ran in carrying a package. Sid opened the box and pulled out an enormous red firework labelled 'The Big One'.

"Extremely dangerous. Keep out of reach of children," Sid read. He looked for something to blow up.

"Hey. Where's that wimpy cowboy doll?" Sid wondered, looking for Woody. Sid's eyes rested on the crate. Sid lifted it up, but Woody wasn't underneath.

Woody clung to the inside of the crate as Sid put it back down. As he searched for Woody, he stepped on Buzz and activated his laser.

"I've always wanted to put a spaceman into orbit," Sid said. He picked up Buzz. Sid put the crate on the workbench and rested his toolbox on top. Woody dropped from the roof of the crate, and hid under a magazine.

Kind-hearted Bo Peep is often the voice of reason for all the toys, and doesn't give up on Woody. **JOHN LEE / DIGITAL**

Woody watched as Sid taped Buzz to the firework. Sid was ready to launch, but a clap of thunder and raindrops pelting his window meant lift-off would have to wait.

"Oh man!" Sid complained, disappointed, before pretending to be a reporter and turning it into part of the game. "Launch of the shuttle has been delayed due to adverse weather conditions at the launch site," Sid announced. "Tomorrow's forecast, sunny."

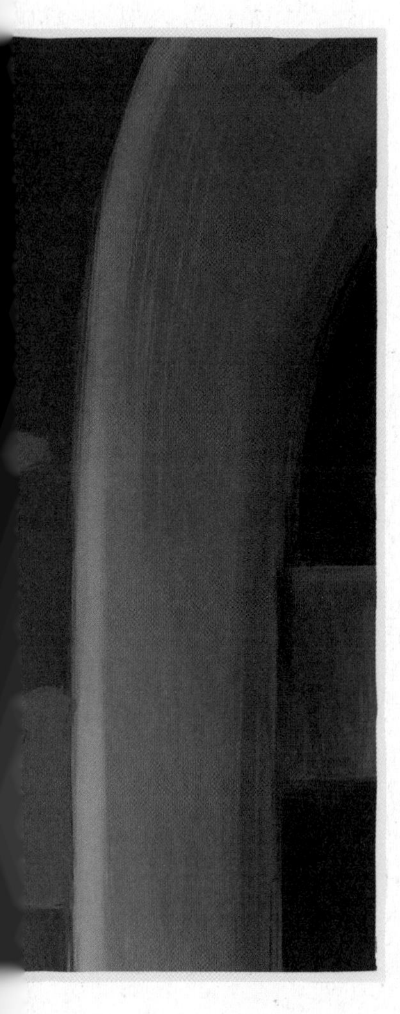

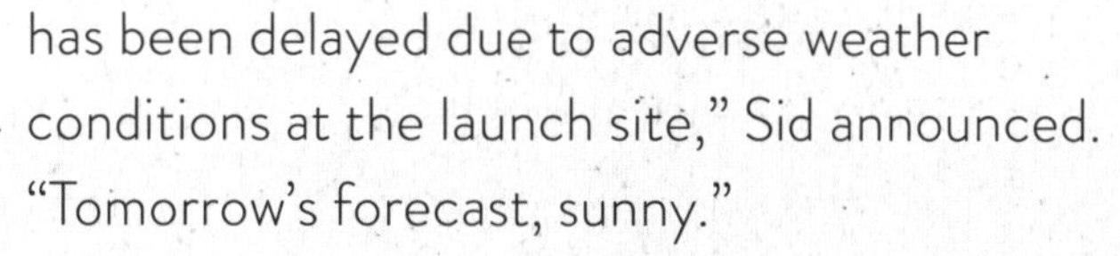

Sid set his alarm clock for the morning and laughed as he said, "Sweet dreams".

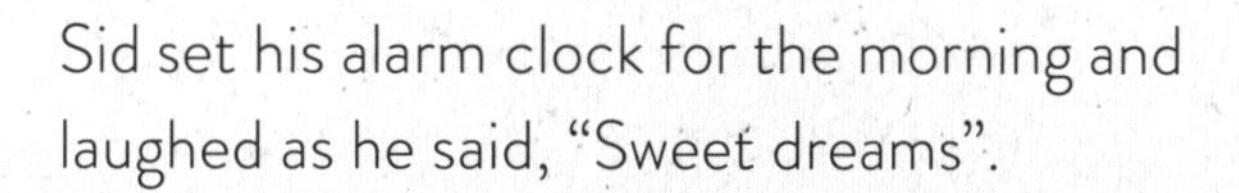

In Andy's room, Andy's mother told him that she had looked everywhere for Woody and Buzz but could only find Andy's cowboy hat. Andy was worried that they'd leave them behind.

"I'm sure we'll find Woody and Buzz before we leave tomorrow," Andy's mother said, kissing him goodnight.

When Andy's mother had left the room, Bo Peep looked over at Andy tucked up in his bed, clutching his beloved cowboy hat.

"Oh Woody," Bo said. "If only you could see how much Andy misses you."

Next door, as Sid slept on his bare mattress, Woody tried to get Buzz's attention. Woody wanted Buzz to take the toolbox off the crate so they could escape, but Buzz didn't move. Woody needed Buzz's help.

"I can't help anyone," Buzz said. Woody said of course he could, and that when he did they could escape to Andy's house. Buzz didn't see the difference between Sid's house and Andy's. Woody thought Buzz mustn't be thinking clearly, but Buzz said he was thinking more clearly now that he knew he was not a space ranger.

"I'm just a toy. A stupid, little, insignificant toy," Buzz said.

Woody reminded him that Andy thought Buzz was the greatest, not because he was a space ranger, but because he was his toy. Buzz didn't see why Andy would want him, but Woody said it was because Buzz was amazing.

Ralph Eggleston's colour story for *Toy Story* provided filmmakers with a visual overview of the film. **Ralph Eggleston / Pastel**

"Look at you. You're a Buzz Lightyear," Woody said. Buzz had wings, glowed in the dark, could talk and had a whooshy helmet. Woody told him that most toys would give anything to be as cool as Buzz. But Woody realised Buzz was too cool. Woody said a cowboy like him didn't stand a chance against Buzz. Woody didn't see why Andy would ever want to play with him, when he had Buzz.

"I'm the one that should be strapped to that rocket," Woody said.

Buzz looked at Andy's name on the sole of his space boot and finally understood that he wasn't just a toy, he was Andy's toy.

"Listen, Buzz, forget about me," Woody said. Woody told Buzz that he should escape while he could, but Buzz wasn't there.

Woody remains optimistic about escaping from Sid's house. **RALPH EGGLESTON / PASTEL**

Babyface is the leader of the mutant toys and is constructed from one of Hannah's baby doll heads atop a crab-like body. **Ralph Eggleston / Pastel**

Woody heard a scraping coming from the top of the crate – it was Buzz pushing the toolbox. Buzz knew they had to escape so they could get back to Andy.

Working together, they soon had the crate in a position for Woody to climb out. Woody called Buzz, but Buzz kept pushing until the crate and toolbox crash landed on Woody.

Buzz checked if Woody was alright. Woody said he was fine. At that moment, the alarm rang and Sid sat up and smiled.

"Time for lift-off!" Sid said. He grabbed Buzz and ran from the room. Woody tried to follow, but ran into Scud at the door. Woody pushed against it to keep him out. With the door now closed, Sid's toys came out of hiding.

"Guys!" Woody called, happy to see them, but the toys scurried away. He pleaded. Woody told them that Buzz was the only friend he had and that he needed their help to stop him being blown to bits. The Baby-faced spider scuttled to the bench and tapped it to signal the toys to gather. Woody smiled and thanked the toys for their help. Woody explained that they might have to break a few rules, but if his plan worked it would help everyone.

In his room, Andy watched sadly as the last of his boxes were wheeled away. He held Buzz's spaceship box in one hand and his cowboy hat in the other, but the toys were not there.

In his yard, Sid was busy building a launch pad for Buzz out of junk he found in his shed.

In Sid's room, Woody sketched out his plan to the mutant toys. When he was sure everyone knew what they had to do, he said it was time to move.

Legs and Ducky hopped into the air vent, and followed it up to the attic. Woody told the Walking Car to wind up Frog, while other toys climbed on top of one another near the door.

In the attic, Legs and Ducky unscrewed the light fixture to the porch. Ducky poked her head out to check the coast was clear. She hooked herself to Legs's reel, who lowered her to the front door. Legs swung Ducky until she could reach the doorbell.

In the bedroom, Woody waited for the doorbell, then shouted it was time to go. Hand-in-the-Box opened Sid's door and Frog whizzed out into the hall. Scud chased Frog downstairs. With Scud gone, Woody and the rest of the mutant toys scooted out of the door on a skateboard.

Downstairs, Hannah opened the door to see who rang, as Frog whizzed outside. Ducky reached down to grab Frog. Legs reeled them to safety as Scud barrelled past Hannah onto the empty porch.

"Stupid dog!" Hannah said, leaving Scud outside. In the kitchen, the toys on the skateboard skidded under the table.

"Lean back!" Woody cried. Woody tipped the nose of the skateboard upwards to leap through the dog flap into a bush in the back yard.

From the bush, Woody saw Buzz taped to the rocket on the crate. Woody signalled to the toys to fan out across the yard.

"Woody!" Buzz called, relieved to see his friend.

Scud, the aggressive bull terrier, is Sid's partner in torturing toys. **RALPH EGGLESTON / PASTEL**

Buzz asked Woody for help, but Woody told him to be quiet. Woody assured him that everything was under control, then collapsed in a heap.

"What are you doing?" Buzz panicked. As Sid approached the launch pad, he spotted Woody on the ground. Sid wondered how Woody had got there, but then threw him on his barbecue to have a cookout. Sid put a match in Woody's holster for later.

Using the matchbox for a radio, Sid confirmed that he had permission to launch and started the countdown. He was about to light the firework, when he heard a voice.

"Reach for the sky," the voice said. Sid looked to see where it came from. "This town ain't big enough for the two of us," the voice recited. Sid walked over to Woody and picked him up. He thought that Woody was busted.

"Who are you calling busted, Buster?" Woody asked. Sid gasped. "We don't like being blown up, Sid," Woody said.

The colourscript follows the emotional arc of the film. The scenes set in Sid's house are darker in tone. **RALPH EGGLESTON / PASTEL**

"We?" Sid said, trembling. Woody told Sid that he spoke for all the toys. Sid looked around the yard as toys crawled out of the sand pit, while others rose from a muddy ditch. Legs lowered Babyface onto Sid's head. Sid screamed, and screamed even louder when Hand-in-a-Box grabbed his ankle.

Sid is the only human in *Toy Story* who knows the toys are alive.
BUD LUCKEY / MARKER

Woody said he would find out if Sid didn't take care of his toys. "So play nice," Woody warned, looking Sid square in the face. Sid ran screaming into the house.

"We did it!" Woody and the toys celebrated together in the yard.

In the house, Sid told Hannah the toys were alive and ran up to his room crying.

In the yard, Woody thanked the toys for all their hard work.

"Woody!" Buzz thanked his friend and the pair shook hands, just as a car horn sounded next door. Andy was leaving.

Woody and Buzz said goodbye to Sid's toys and ducked through the fence to Andy's driveway, just as the car pulled away.

Woody ran after the car and climbed onto the bumper. He was about to pop open the rear window, when he saw Buzz stuck in the fence.

Buzz told Woody he would catch him up. But Woody hopped down and ran back to help Buzz. Once free, Buzz and Woody chased after the car, but they weren't quick enough. Standing in the middle of the road, Buzz and Woody were almost flattened by a lorry. It was the removal van.

"Come on!" Buzz said, chasing after it. From Sid's porch, Scud saw the toys running and joined in the chase. Buzz caught hold of a strap dangling from the back of the truck.

"You can do it, Woody!" Buzz cried. Woody made a leap and caught it. He started to climb. When he was almost there, Woody looked back and saw Scud. Scud leapt at Woody. Buzz told him to hold on, but Scud was too strong. Woody told Buzz to take care of Andy.

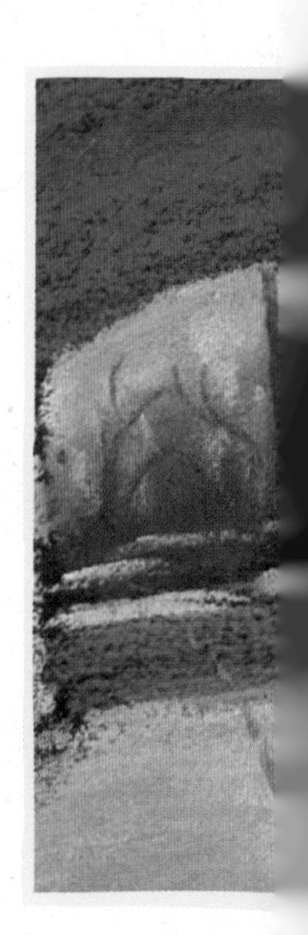

The removals company, Eggman Movers, is named after Pixar's art director Ralph Eggleston. **Ralph Eggleston / Pastel**

But Buzz didn't want to leave without Woody. Buzz leapt onto Scud's nose and made him let go.

Woody rode away with the truck. Suddenly, it stopped at a traffic light. Woody crashed into the door, which opened upwards, taking Woody with it. High above the contents of the van, Woody spotted a box marked 'Andy's Toys'.

Down the street, Scud threw Buzz under a parked car. In the van, Woody tore open the box. "There you are!" Woody said, pulling out RC Car.

Woody took the car to the back of the truck and threw it into the street. The toys screamed in horror. Woody steered RC over to Buzz. RC revved its engines when it saw him. Buzz jumped onto RC Car and raced after them with Scud in hot pursuit.

In the truck Rocky, Andy's wrestler toy, picked up Woody. As Rocky spun Woody around, RC Car turned circles in the street behind the truck. When Rocky threw Woody to the floor, RC Car drove straight.

Hamm leapt on Woody, who nudged the controls. RC Car and Buzz leapt into the air and Buzz landed on the car, facing backwards. The moving van stopped at a red light and Buzz and the remote-controlled car crashed into the back. Scud chased after them. A car swerved to avoid him. Buzz and RC emerged unhurt, but Scud was surrounded by angry drivers.

In the van, the toys lifted Woody into the air. "Wait!" Woody begged, but the toys tossed him out of the back.

After almost getting run over, Buzz and RC Car picked Woody up. Woody switched RC into turbo mode.

RC Car's design evolved from the red seen here to green and blue. **RALPH EGGLESTON / PASTEL**

Loyal Slinky Dog stretches to breaking point while trying to rescue Buzz and Woody. **JILL CULTON / PENCIL**

In the moving van, Lenny spotted RC Car. Bo Peep picked up Lenny and saw Buzz and Woody. Woody had been telling the truth! Bo Peep told Rocky to lower the ramp so Woody and Buzz could drive RC aboard. Rocky pushed on the lever and the ramp came down hard.

Slinky told the toys to grab onto his tail as he stretched towards Woody and Buzz. Woody reached to grab Slinky's paw. Woody thanked Slinky, but RC started to slow down. Slinky told Woody to speed up, but Buzz said the batteries were running low.

"Whoa!" Slinky cried as RC started to swerve and he stretched even further. Slinky couldn't hold on much longer. As RC Car slowed down even more, Woody's hands slipped from Slinky's grasp. Buzz, Woody and RC ground to a halt.

"Great!" Woody muttered, annoyed.

"Woody, the rocket!" Buzz said. Then Woody remembered the match in his holster. He struck the match against the tyre. Woody was about to light the firework when a car rushed past, and blew it out. He looked at the smoking match.

"No! No! No!" Woody fell to his knees. He felt something warm on the back of his hand. Woody looked, and saw a circle of light starting to smoke. Buzz's helmet was concentrating the sunlight on the back of his hand, just like Sid's magnifying glass. Woody grabbed the fuse of the firework and positioned Buzz so that his helmet concentrated the light onto the end. The fuse burst into flame.

"You did it!" Buzz cheered as he climbed back onto the car. Suddenly it dawned on Woody that rockets explode. Buzz and Woody held on tight as the firework whooshed them down the busy street.

With the help of 'The Big One' rocket, Buzz finally flies. **Ralph Eggleston / Pastel**

In the truck, Slinky was blaming himself for not holding on longer, when Lenny called out that Woody and Buzz were coming up fast. Buzz held onto Woody and RC tightly as they raced through the air behind the truck, but just as they reached it, Buzz lost control. Woody let go of RC who shot into the back of the truck while he and Buzz zoomed high into the air. Woody told Buzz that this was the part when they blew up.

"Not today," Buzz said. He pressed his red button to release his wings. Buzz's wings sliced through the tape. The firework exploded, while Buzz and Woody fell to the ground.

Woody covered his eyes as the earth rushed towards them, but when he uncovered them he found that he, or rather Buzz, was flying.

"You're flying!" Woody marvelled. But Buzz said he was falling with style.

Buzz swooped towards the moving van, but passed over the roof. Woody told Buzz they had missed it, but Buzz wasn't aiming for the truck. Buzz flew on towards the open sunroof of Andy's mother's car. Buzz and Woody clattered down into an open box sitting beside Andy.

"Wow!" Andy cried. Andy told his mother he had found Woody and Buzz in the back of the car.

"Now what'd I tell you?" Andy's mom said. "Right where you left them."

Buzz gave Woody a wink just before they froze, safe in Andy's arms.

***

The following Christmas, in his new house, Andy opened presents around the tree with his family, while Sarge hid with the baby monitor among the decorations to report back to Andy's toys.

In Andy's room, Buzz sat on the edge of Andy's bed, listening to the receiver.

"It's time," Rex said as the toys gathered round. Woody rushed to join them but was stopped by Bo Peep who looped her crook around his neck to kiss him under the mistletoe.

On the bed, the toys listened to the soldiers' broadcast. The first gift was for Molly and was a Mrs Potato Head. Mr Potato Head was delighted and pulled off his moustache to look smart for his new bride.

Sarge was about to announce the next toy when the radio began to crackle. Buzz banged the monitor.

The toys asked Buzz if he was worried. They wondered what Andy could get that was better than a Buzz Lightyear. They soon found out, as Andy's delighted voice cried out, "A puppy!"

New best friends Woody and Buzz are delighted to be reunited with Andy. **JILL CULTON / PENCIL**

The Art of Pixar Toy Story

Toy Story, the first instalment in the popular film franchise, was Pixar's first feature film as well as the world's first entirely computer-animated feature film. John Lasseter made his directorial debut after Pixar was approached by Disney to produce a computer-animated feature film told from a toy's perspective.

Despite the film being computer-animated, the development of the film included thousands of pieces of art from character sketches and concept paintings through to the colourscripts, many of which are seen throughout this book. Ralph Eggleston created the colourscript for *Toy Story* – spending a week or so illustrating a series of postage-stamp sized images showcasing each scene in the story. Lasseter was impressed with Eggleston's work which allowed the team at Pixar to see the colour, lighting and emotional arc of the film – an essential tool in planning the visual rhythm of the story.

Toy Story was released in 1995 and received three Academy Award nominations. Ten years later, the film was selected for preservation in the United States National Film Registry by the Library of Congress.

Woody and Buzz race towards the removal van by putting RC into turbo mode. **Bob Pauley / Marker and Pencil**

Pixar Studio Artists

Ralph Eggleston

Concept art on pages 4, 11, 15, 16, 17, 21, 22, 30–31, 52, 64 and 68–69. Colour story on pages 26–27, 29, 38, 41, 42, 44–45, 46, 50, 51, 54–55, 56–57, 58–59, 60 and 62–63.

Bud Luckey

Concept art on pages 4, 13, 17, 19, 23, 28, 39, 40, 43 and 57.

Lou Fancher

Concept art on pages 8–9 and 36–37.

Steve Johnson

Concept art on pages 8–9 and 36–37.

Tia W. Kratter

Concept art on pages 11 and 68–69.

Michael Yates

Concept art on page 12.

Joe Ranft

Concept art on page 14.

Bob Pauley

Concept art on pages 20, 24, 47 and 66.

Dan Haskett

Concept art on page 25.

Bill Cone

Concept art on page 32.

Kelly Asbury

Concept art on page 34.

Jason Katz

Concept art on page 35.

John Lee

Concept art on pages 48–49.

Jill Culton

Concept art on pages 61 and 64.

Andy's room is instantly recognisable with its white cloud wallpaper which has become a symbol of the *Toy Story films*. **TIA W. KRATTER AND RALPH EGGLESTON / ACRYLIC**